J. H. Bryson

Scotch-Irish Addresses

The Scotch-Irish people

J. H. Bryson

Scotch-Irish Addresses
The Scotch-Irish people

ISBN/EAN: 9783337409814

Printed in Europe, USA, Canada, Australia, Japan

Cover: Foto ©Andreas Hilbeck / pixelio.de

More available books at **www.hansebooks.com**

SCOTCH-IRISH ADDRESSES.

THE SCOTCH-IRISH PEOPLE.

THEIR INFLUENCE IN THE FORMATION OF THE GOVERNMENT OF
THE UNITED STATES OF AMERICA. DELIVERED AT
THE THIRD CONGRESS, HELD AT LOUIS-
VILLE, KY., MAY 14, 1891.

INVENTORS OF THE SCOTCH-IRISH RACE
OF AMERICA.

DELIVERED AT THE FOURTH CONGRESS, HELD AT ATLANTA, GA.,
ON THE 28TH DAY OF APRIL, 1892.

BY REV. J. H. BRYSON, D.D.,
Huntsville, Ala.

NASHVILLE, TENN.:
PUBLISHING HOUSE OF THE METHODIST EPISCOPAL CHURCH, SOUTH.
BARBEE & SMITH, AGENTS.
1892.

THE SCOTCH-IRISH PEOPLE:

THEIR INFLUENCE IN THE FORMATION OF THE GOVERNMENT OF THE UNITED STATES.

BY J. H. BRYSON, D.D.

THE science of government is a study full of interest from every stand-point of investigation. The nature and genius of a government cannot be correctly understood without a clear apprehension of the several elements which enter into the formation of the governmental structure. There are always antecedents of a marked and pronounced character, which lead up to every great historical epoch, and these great events of human history must be carefully studied in the light of these antecedents if they are to be properly understood.

The formation of the government of the United States is the grandest and most distinguished achievement of human history. It has no parallel in any age or century. It is the outgrowth of principles, which had to work their way through long periods of suffering and conflict. The logical and regulative structure of the principles of our government into an instrument, which we call our Constitution, was the result of but a few months' labor; the principles themselves, however, had been struggling through martyrdom and blood for many generations. To understand the government of the United States, the genius and character of the people who settled the several colonies must be carefully studied. Its most distinguishing feature is that it is a government framed by the people for the people. It is their own conception of the best form of government to secure personal right and liberty.

In the present discourse we propose to review the influence which the Scotch-Irish people exerted in various ways in the formation of our government. The inhabitants of the colonies up to 1776 were almost entirely an English-speaking people, coming from England, Scotland, and Ireland. The French Huguenot was not a large element in the settlement of the country, but it was a most important one. There was also a noble body of settlers from Holland. These different classes of people all have an honorable part, worthy of themselves, in forming the government of our country.

When the government of the United States came into existence, as the voice of the people speaking through thirteen sovereign States, the world stood amazed at the daring and brilliant conception. Tyranny and oppression received a fatal blow in that glorious day, and human liberty found a permanent home in the hearts of three millions of American citizens. Many were the prophecies of its speedy downfall, but with the first century of its history it has taken the first place among the nations of the world. The principles of this government are no longer a matter of experiment, but, as a distinguished writer has said: "they are believed to disclose and display the type of institutions toward which, as by a law of fate, the rest of civilized mankind are forced to move, some with swifter, others with slower, but all with unhesitating feet."*

The causes which led to the formation of the American Government were foreign to the people of the colonies. They did not willingly break allegiance with the mother country. It was the oppressive measures of the British Crown which forced them to declare their independence and construct a new government, if they would be freemen. But the birthday of constitutional liberty had come. A mysterious providence had prepared a people, through long years of suffering and trial, for the glorious heritage, and had held in reserve a magnificent continent for their abiding-place. The era of 1776 was not within the range of human conception or forecast, but there was above and behind it all a divine Mind, bringing forward the day with all its stupendous revelations.

In considering the history of any people, it is a serious defect to leave out of view their religious conceptions, as expressed in their formulas of faith. Religion of necessity is the most powerful factor in the direction of human life. Mr. Carlyle has well said: "A man's religion is the chief fact with regard to him."† In a Christian land, with an open Bible, this is pre-eminently true. With the American colonies religious liberty was a question of not less vital importance than that of civil liberty. Their religious faith had a most powerful influence in forming their character, and they intend to be untrammeled in its exercise. From New Hampshire to Georgia they were Calvinists of the most pronounced type. Calvinism was their religious creed, and out of it sprung their political principles. This had been the creed of their ancestors from the days of the Reformation. It had stood the test of fire and sword for more than two hundred years. The principles of that wonderful system had permeated their whole being.

* Brice's "American Commonwealth," Volume I., page 1.
† Carlyle's "Heroes," page 1.

It gave them intellectual strength and vigor. It intensified to the highest degree their individuality. It developed that integrity and force of character, which no blandishments or persecutions could break down. He who puts a light estimate upon Calvinism knows little of its principles, and he knows little of the struggles which brave Calvinists have made in many lands for freedom. Motley speaks correctly when he says: " Holland, England, and America owe their liberties to Calvinists." Ranke, the great German historian, as well as D'Aubigne, says: " Calvin was the true founder of the American Government." Hume, Macaulay, Buckle, Froude, and Leckey all affirm that it was the stern, unflinching courage of the Calvinistic Puritan that won the priceless heritage of English liberty. Scotland can never estimate what she owes John Knox, the fearless embodiment of Calvinism in Church and State. Mr. Bancroft makes the statement conspicuous that it was the Calvinistic faith of the American colonies, which prompted them to resist the oppressions of the British Crown, and maintain the desperate struggle with unfaltering courage until the glorious victory was achieved.

The distinguishing feature of Calvinism as a theology is its representative character, holding that sin and guilt are the result of representation in Adam, and that redemption is the result of representation in Christ. The logical outworking of such a theology is a representative government, both in Church and State. Calvinism is the chief corner-stone of the American Republic.

It was the religious faith of the colonies that made them what they were, and no adequate conception of their resistance to oppression or their struggle for freedom can be had if this fact is left out of view. The settlers of the American colonies were worthy sons of noble sires. Their ancestors in the plantations of Ulster, in Scotland, in England, in Holland, and in France had learned from their Calvinistic faith that resistance to tyranny was service to God. Calvinism is sometimes looked upon as a stern and severe religious faith, still it is the faith which has produced the grandest men and women the world has ever known. This is the faith which breasted for centuries the most terrible conflicts, trials, and sufferings, to secure for us the glorious heritage of constitutional liberty. Of these heroes Mr. Froude has well said: " They were splintered and torn, but they ever bore an inflexible front to illusion and mendacity, and preferred rather to be ground to powder like flint, than to bend before violence, or melt before enervating temptation." *

* St. Andrew's "Address on Calvinism."

In the memorable revolution of 1776, when the American colonies combined to form a government of their own, the Scotch-Irish people, who formed a large part of the settlers of the central and southern colonies, bore a conspicuous part. In speaking of the Scotch-Irish people as transplanted from Ulster, in Ireland, to America, we have found it impossible to separate the Scotch and the Scotch-Irish. They are really one people. During the persecutions in Ireland, thousands of this people were forced to return to Scotland, and at a later date many of them emigrated to America. Often parts of the same families in Scotland and Ireland would join each other in the colonies. This is true of the Livingstons, the Hamiltons, the Wilsons, the Witherspoons, the Randolphs, the Grahams, and others. There is still another mixture in the veins of the Scotch-Irish people. Many of them are known to be of Huguenot ancestry. The Caldwells, the Dunlaps, the Brysons, the Duffields, the Pickenses, the Sumpters, and others came from France to Scotland, thence to Ireland, and thence to America.

In estimating the influence of the Scotch-Irish in the formation of the government of the United States two questions may be asked: What was their religious creed? and what were their political ideas? Their religious faith was Calvinism; in Church government they were Presbyterians; in State government they were republicans. These three ideas make Scotch-Irishmen what they are. Always and everywhere they are the fearless and unflinching advocates of liberty, the determined and unfaltering foe of oppression. They are by nature bold, courageous, and aggressive people.

At the time of the American Revolution, the Scotch-Irish people must have formed near one-third of the entire population of the colonies. The tide of emigration became strong in the early part of the eighteenth century. As early as 1725, a large body of this people had settled in almost every colony. From this time onward, for a period of more than forty years, the steady flow of this people to the American colonies was something amazing. For many years there were never less than 12,000 landed annually at the different ports of the country; and for the two years after the Antrim evictions it is estimated the numbers ran up to 30,000 or more. They settled generally in the central and southern colonies. Some 20,000 or more, however, settled along the coast from Boston to the mouth of the Kennebec. This distribution of the Scotch-Irish over the whole country made it possible for them to exert a most powerful influence when the occasion should arise. So soon as they were settled down in their new homes they organized themselves into Churches and Presbyteries (for they were Presbyterians), and in 1717 a General Synod was formed. By 1770, this delegated Synod was the most powerful religious organization in the country. Indeed, it was the only organization which embraced all the colonies. The ministry were an able body of men, graduates of Edinburgh, Glasgow, Dublin, Harvard, Yale, and Princeton. Many of the elders were graduates of these institutions. This General Synod, with delegates coming from almost every colony, met every year under a written Constitution which they had adopted. This compact organization of able men, coming together annually as delegates from the territory of the several colonies, for a period of more than fifty years, was certainly a most powerful agency in preparing the way for a Congress of all the colonies when the occasion should arise. This General Synod of the Presbyterian Church, which was the only representative body of the whole country, was very obnoxious to the British Crown, and the Governors of the larger colonies were instructed to remonstrate against its assembling. But these Presbyterians knew their rights and had the courage to maintain them. In May, 1775, this General Synod of the Presbyterian Church met in Philadelphia, side by side with the Colonial Congress. It was a critical period. The Congress seemed to hesitate what to do. The Presbyterian Synod, made up of Scotch-Irish, bravely and courageously met the issue. The famous " Pastoral Letter "* was issued by that body to their Churches scattered throughout the colonies, to adhere to the resolutions of the Congress, and to make earnest prayer to God for guidance in all measures looking to the defense of the country. This powerful letter was scattered broadcast among the people, and a copy was sent to the Legislature of every colony. The people were everywhere aroused to the profound significance of the crisis which was upon them. This Philadelphia Synod and their circular letter are referred to by Adolphus in his work on the "Reign of George the Third," as the chief cause which led the colonies to determine on resistance. The Scotch-Irish people, by their Annual Synod assembling for fifty or sixty years, manifestly prepared the way for the *union of the colonies in a Colonial Congress*, so that they might jointly inaugurate measures to protect their common interests. In that distinguished body which assembled in 1774, men of Scotch-Irish blood held an honorable place. There were the Livingstons, of New York ; John Sullivan, of New Hampshire ; Dickenson and McKean, of Pennsylvania ; Patrick Henry, of Virginia ; and the Rutledges, of South Carolina ; and others—men whose ability and culture would adorn any position.

*" Presbyterians and the Revolution," page 121.

This union of the colonies enabled them to realize their power and strength. They petitioned the Crown and Parliament for a redress of their wrongs. But their petitions were unheeded. The conflict was inevitable. On the 4th of July, 1776, the memorable Declaration of Independence was made, and the bold announcement went forth to the world that the American colonies intended to be a free and independent people. The grandest hour of human history had come. The heaven-born principles of constitutional liberty had found a home in the breasts of three millions of people; and a continent—the very paradise of the earth—was to be the permanent resting-place. The history of that immortal day is ever full of thrilling interest to the sons of liberty. The Continental Congress fully realized the tremendous issues involved in that declaration. Behind them were the throbbing hearts of a united people awaiting with intense anxiety for the deed to be done. It was an hour that was to mark the grandest epoch in human history. What a scene was there! On the table in the presence of that able body of statesmen lay the charter of human freedom, its clear-cut utterances flinging defiance in the face of oppression, and proclaiming to the world that America was henceforth the asylum of freemen. It was an hour when strong men trembled. But the anxious silence was broken when the venerable Dr. Witherspoon, in whose veins flowed the best blood of our race, arose and uttered the thrilling words: " To hesitate at this moment is to consent to our own slavery. That noble instrument upon your table, which insures immortality to its author, should be subscribed this very morning by every pen in this house. He that will not respond to its accents and strain every nerve to carry into effect its provisions is unworthy the name of freeman. Whatever I may have of property or reputation is staked on the issue of this contest; and although these gray hairs must soon descend into the sepulcher, I would infinitely rather that they descend hither by the hand of the executioner than desert at this crisis the sacred cause of my country." *

These burning words from one of the most distinguished leaders of the Congress carried the matter to a triumphant conclusion: the Declaration of Independence was signed, and the foundation of the American Government was laid.

This action of Congress was hailed with universal rejoicings by the people, although they knew full well it would involve them in a terrible and bloody conflict with the British Crown.

As to the influence which foreshadowed this memorable event, it can-

* " Presbyterians and the Revolution," page 166.

not be said that it was wholly brought about by any single cause; but
the historical writers who speak of this period are free to say that a
large proportion of the great leaders who influenced the colonies to
take this decisive step were men of Scotch-Irish blood. "Patrick
Henry, of Virginia," said Mr. Jefferson, "was far ahead of us all; he
led the way, and the people from the sea-board to the mountains were
aroused to action by his burning words." David Caldwell, Ephraim
Brevard, Alexander Craighead, and James Hall, with their worthy associates, had the people of North Carolina educated far in advance of
the Colonial Congress, as the famous Mecklenburg Declaration illus-
trated. The two Rutledges, the eloquent Tennant, and others kindled
the patriotic fires in South Carolina. Duffield, Wilson, Smith, and
Thomas Craighead, with their noble associates, prepared the people of
Pennsylvania for the coming conflict. The action of the citizens of
Westmoreland and Cumberland Counties, with that of Hanna's Town,
in May, 1776, told what fearless patriotism the burning words of these
courageous leaders had enkindled. The people of New Jersey, under
the teaching of Dr. Witherspoon, were ready and impatiently waiting
for the hour. Read and McKean were the brave leaders in Delaware.
Smith, Rodgers, and Livingston, with their famous " Whig Club," con-
trolled the sentiment of New York. Thornton and Sullivan were leaders of the people of New Hampshire, and already had their forces fighting in the field. These all were Scotch-Irishmen, leading and forming
public opinion everywhere. The Governors of the central and southern colonies were not far wrong when they informed the home government that the Presbyterian (or Scotch-Irish) clergy were to blame for
bringing about the Revolution, and that it was their fiery zeal which
instigated the people to resistance. That the Scotch-Irish clergy exerted a most powerful influence upon the people, by their constant and
faithful instruction in the principles of religious and civil liberty, is
unquestionably true. How could it be otherwise? On the walls of
their homes hung the " National Covenants " of Scotland, which many
of their ancestors had signed with their blood. These famous and his-
toric covenants form the rugged and storm-beaten background, on
which came out the glorious Declaration of American Independence.
The brave, thrilling words of that immortal instrument tell what important lessons the author had learned from his maternal ancestry.
Ephraim Brevard and Thomas Jefferson wrote alike. They drank at
the same fountain; they had the same instructor. It can be said, without fear of challenge, that Scotch-Irish blood flows through every prin-

ciple written in the declaration which forms the foundation of American liberty.

It is a common statement of history that the clergy of the colonies were in advance of any other class in urging resistance to the oppressive legislation of the mother country. The Scotch-Irish clergy, being dissenters, were untrammeled, and bravely did they speak out in defense of their country's right. The published sermons of that day show how ably the ministry labored to form a public opinion that would stand up against every form of tyranny and despotism.

At that period no single agency in the country had such tremendous power as the pulpit. The ministry were universally a highly educated class. They were Calvinists in their creed, and they had learned their principles of liberty from the word of God. They put the issue upon the highest ground. They taught the people that resistance to tyrants was a duty to God. Their courageous words led the people irresistibly onward. "Arm for freedom's cause, appeal to the God of battles, and go forward," was their thrilling appeal sweeping through all the land. Gloriously was their work accomplished when " Independence Bell " rang out the dawn of freedom's day.

The public declaration of the colonies that they had severed their allegiance to the British Crown, all understood must bring on a fierce and bitter war; indeed, Washington, with his armies, was already in the field, and the battle had begun. Rapidly the colonists transformed themselves into sovereign States; and, taking the reins of government into their own hands, elected their own Legislatures and Governors. That seven of the first Governors of the thirteen States should be men of Scotch-Irish blood is an honored tribute to that noble race. This proud distinction indicates the high estimate in which this people were held at the very beginning of the American Revolution. In the long protracted war waged by England to recover her revolted colonies the Scotch-Irish people bore a prominent and honorable part. A large number of the most distinguished officers of the army of every rank were of this people. Gens. Knox, Wayne, Montgomery, Sullivan, Mercer, Starke, Morgan, Davidson, and many others were conspicuous for their heroic deeds and efficient services on many battlefields.

In the earlier days of the revolution occurred the famous battle of Saratoga, in which the entire British army was captured. This decisive victory, defeating the well-conceived strategic movement to cut the colonies in twain, has been justly regarded as the great turning-point in American affairs, and, as a leading English historian says, changing the whole current of future history.* It was this important event which secured the alliance of France, the recognition of Spain and Holland, besides bringing to the surface a favorable sentiment in England. Two brave Scotch-Irish officers, Col. Morgan and Col. Starke, contributed largely if not chiefly to this result. Knowing the importance of checking the invasion from Canada under Burgoyne, Gen. Washington organized a regiment of picked riflemen, placed it in command of Col. Morgan, and dispatched it to the support of Gen. Gates. On the morning of the 7th of October, 1777, the two armies met for a decisive struggle. Col. Morgan commanded the left wing of the American forces, being confronted by Gen. Frazer with the flower of the British army. After fighting had continued fiercely for several hours, Frazer fell by the deadly aim of Morgan's riflemen; and, seeing their commander borne from the field, the whole British line gave way, and the great battle of the war was won. Col. Starke, who had already defeated a strong force at Bennington, seized the fords of the Hudson, thereby compelling the surrender of the entire British army. The whole country was electrified by the victory, and the daring bravery of Morgan and Starke were universally applauded.

During the prosecution of the war the settlements in Western Pennsylvania and Virginia and the new settlements in Kentucky were continually threatened and imperiled by Indian raids, sent out by English officers from the line of forts between the lakes and the Mississippi River. Col. Rogers Clarke, a brave, daring Scotch-Irishman, conceived the idea of organizing a secret force to capture these dangerous outposts. He unfolded his bold conception to Gov. Henry, of Virginia, and obtained a commission to collect a body of trusty riflemen, and such supplies as might be needed. He selected men of his own race, hardy, courageous, and true. They went forth upon their daring mission determined to succeed or perish in the attempt. The expedition was a brilliant success: Gov. Hamilton, with his line of forts, was surprised and captured. The broad sweep of country from the Ohio to the lakes was conquered, and it was the magnificent contribution of a few brave Scotch-Irishmen to the government of the United States.

When the British generals, after a number of manoeuvers and various engagements, failed to dislodge General Washington from his strong position in the hill region of New Jersey, they turned their attion to the southern part of the country. Lord Cornwallis was in command, and marching northward from Charleston, he met and de-

---

* Creasy's "Fifteen Decisive Battles," page 376.

feated the colonial forces under General Gates at Camden, which virtually gave him control of South Carolina. He then advanced his
position to Charlotte and Salisbury, North Carolina, his purpose being
to pass rapidly through that State to the southern part of Virginia.
Suddenly, however, a strong body of Scotch-Irishmen from the valleys
of the Watauga and the Holston, under the leadership of Campbell,
Shelby, and Sevier, joined by Williams and Cleaveland, of South
Carolina, appeared upon the field. They were a bold, fearless body of
riflemen. Gloom, distress, and almost despair, had settled upon the
Southern colonies. Cornwallis had reported to the British Government that the whole Southern country was subjugated. In a few days
came the battle of King's Mountain. Ferguson was killed, and the
entire command was captured. It was a Scotch-Irishmen's battle,
made at their own suggestion, when they heard the enemy were ad-
vancing into the up country. Hope and courage revived everywhere.
The Southland was the home of the Scotch-Irish, and they were prompt
and ready to defend it at every cost. This brilliant victory proved
to be the turning-point of the war in the South, and it was really the
beginning of the end. Three months later, and only a few miles from
the same place, General Morgan, the hero of Saratoga, fought the
famous battle of the Cowpens, completely routing Tarleton's entire
command, and inflicting a most disastrous blow upon the British
army.

This brilliant victory of General Morgan and his Scotch-Irish troops
thrilled the whole country with rejoicing. General Davidson, of North
Carolina, wrote that the victory " gladdened every countenance and
paved the way for the salvation of the country." The State of Virginia voted General Morgan a horse and sword in testimony of the
" highest esteem of his country for his military character and abilities
so gloriously displayed." Congress placed on record the " most
lively sense of approbation of the conduct of General Morgan and the
men and officers under his command;"* also voting him a gold medal,
inscribing upon it the terse but complimentary words. " Virtus unita
valet:" " United virtue prevails." Of the effect of this signal victory
upon the country Lord Cornwallis wrote to General Clinton, the commander in chief of the British forces in America: " It is impossible to
foresee all the consequences that this unexpected and extraordinary
event may produce." "As the defeat of Ferguson at King's Mountain
made to Cornwallis the first invasion of North Carolina impossible, so

---

* Bancroft's "History of the United States," Volume V., page 484.

Tarleton foresaw that the battle of Cowpens would make the second disastrous." These two decisive victories, won by the heroic valor and patriotism of men of Scotch-Irish blood, foreshadowed the coming surrender of Yorktown. It was the hour when the fatal handwriting came out upon the wall, pointing England to the inevitable result. In her folly she had sown to the wind; in her bitterness she must reap the whirlwind.

Mr. Bancroft, the cultured historian of the American revolution, in referring to this last distinguished service which General Morgan rendered to his country, sums up his career in this forcible language: "Appointed by Congress at the outbreak of hostilities a Captain of Provincials, he raised a body of riflemen and marched from the valley of Virginia to Boston in twenty-one days. He commanded the van in the fearful march through the wilderness to Canada. Thrice he led a forlorn hope before Quebec. To him belongs the chief glory of the first great engagement with Burgoyne's army, and he shared in all that followed till the surrender; and now he had won at the Cowpens the most astounding victory of the war. Forced into retirement by ill health brought on by exposure, he took with him the praises of all the army, and of the chief civil representatives of the country. He was at the time the ablest commander of light troops in the world. In no European army of that day were there troops like those that he trained. The corps under him so partook of his spirit that they were fashioned into one life, one energy, and one action." *

In reviewing the different influences which worked jointly and so successfully to the achievement of American independence we are persuaded that the American clergy have not yet received at the hands of an enlightened public sentiment that tribute of recognition and praise, to which their distinguished services so justly entitled them. Mr. Headley, in his attractive little volume "The Chaplains and Clergy of the Revolution," has done something to vindicate the memory of these noble and godly men, who stood bravely up for their country's right in that perilous day.

He begins his little work with these significant words: "Notwithstanding the numberless books that have been written on the American Revolution, there is one feature of it which has been overlooked. I mean the religious element. In this respect there is not a single history of that great struggle which is not so radically defective as to render the charge against it of incompleteness a valid one. And he who for-

* Bancroft's "History of the United States," Volume V., pages 488, 480.

gets or underestimates the moral forces that uphold or bear on a great struggle lacks the chief qualities of an historian." * In speaking of the American clergy on the present occasion and the part they bore in the great struggle of the Revolution, we are restricted of course to those who belong to the Scotch-Irish race. The ministers who were of this blood were almost without exception Presbyterians, and without exception, too, they were stanch supporters of the cause of American liberty. Having urged resistance to the unjust legislation of the British Crown, they were not wanting in the hour when the conflict came. Being men of liberal culture and thoroughly conversant with the issues involved in the struggle, it is not surprising that their influence was great among the people. No class of men did so much to fire the popular heart with a determined spirit of resistance.

Craighead, McWhirter, Hall, Tennant, and others, all ministers, were sent into different sections of the country to arouse and stir the people to action in the great crisis. Many of them raised companies and regiments and courageously led them in battle. Many were chaplains in the army; and when reverses and depressions came, it was their stirring appeals which kept the patriotic fires burning, and awakened fresh courage for a renewed struggle. They served in almost every capacity. They were in Legislatures, in State conventions, in councils of safety, in all positions which required wisdom, vigor, and decision. Washington knew the value of these distinguished men as counselors. Witherspoon, Rodgers, McWhirter, Caldwell, and Duffield were often in conference with him in the darkest days of the Revolution. He knew he had their sympathies, and he had respect for their judgment. He sometimes risked important movements on their information about places, persons, and surroundings, and they never failed him.

Rev. Dr. Witherspoon, of Princeton, was one of the most conspicuous characters of this period. He served in the Continental Congress for a number of years, and it was conceded that he had no superior in that distinguished body. He was a member of every important committee, and his influence was recognized as a most potent factor in guiding the government safely through that stormy period.

Tennant, of Charleston, was the close associate of the Rutledges, the Pinkneys, Drayton, and Gadsden; they knew his strength and sought his counsel. He was a member of the State convention, and it was his powerful influence with the people which aroused them from their lethargy, when brave men feared all was lost.

* Headley's "Chaplains and Clergy of the Revolution," pages 13, 14.

Turning to New Jersey, we find the Rev. James Caldwell the popular idol of the State. As chaplain of the First Brigade, he kept the enthusiasm of the troops to the highest pitch. When reverses came, his resolute spirit rose with the hour. He flung despondency to the winds, giving encouragement to all by his cheering words. When the supplies of the army were running short, and all efforts to secure them were unavailing, he was induced to accept the position of Assistant Commissary General. Such was his indomitable energy and his personal favor with all classes that he soon had the army amply supplied. To him the general officers looked continuously for reliable information about the enemy. He seemed ubiquitous, and nothing could escape his keen, penetrating scrutiny. Washington esteemed his service invaluable. The invading force could keep nothing concealed from his incessant watchfulness. His own vigorous enthusiasm he imparted to the people everywhere. He seemed by intuition to know the plans of the enemy, and so often did he thwart their plans and purposes in their inception, that a large price was offered for his capture. On one occasion he ventured to his home, aiming to get his family out of the way of the frequent raids of the enemy. Apprised of his coming, the Hessian troopers made an effort to capture him; but failing in their designs, they murdered his wife in the presence of her children, firing the manse over them, and only the prompt efforts of neighbors saved the little children and the dead body of the mother from the flames. It was a fearful blow to the husband and father. His sufferings seemed, however, if possible, to give him greater influence with the army and the people. The best families of the State asked the privilege of caring for his motherless children. Lafayette adopted one of his sons, and gave him the love and opportunities of his princely home. His trials increased, rather than relaxed, his energies in the varied offices in which he served. When the battle came, he was always with the soldiers in the thickest of the fight. On one occasion, in a hot engagement at the village of Springfield, he discovered the fire of one of the companies slackened for want of wadding; he quickly rushed into a Presbyterian church near by, gathered an armful of Watts's hymn books, distributed them along the line, and said: "Now put Watts into them, boys." With a laugh and a cheer they rammed the charges home, and gave the British Watts with a will.

The upper part of New Jersey being a strong strategic position, Gen. Washington kept a strong force there continuously; and the important service of Mr. Caldwell, until the day he fell by the hand of an assassin, it would be impossible to overstate. "He was a man of un-

wearied activity, and wonderful powers. Feelings of the most glow-
ing piety and the most fervent patriotism occupied his bosom at the
same time, without interfering with each other. He was one day
preaching to the battalion; the next, providing ways and means for
their support; and the next, marching with them in battle. If defeated, assisting in the most efficient way to conduct their retreat; if vic-
torious, offering their united thanksgiving to God, and the next day
carrying the consolations of the gospel to some afflicted or dying par-
ishioner." *

Would that time would permit the mention of other clergymen—
Evans, Rogers, Allen, Kerr, Cummins, David Caldwell, Patillo, Alexander Craighead—all belonging to this patriotic race, who wrought
with great power and efficiency in the struggle for American independence!

When a careful review is made of the powerful and influential
causes which led to the successful achievement of our national rights
and liberties, we are persuaded no single influence will stand out with
greater prominence than that of the American clergy.

We have spoken of statesmen, of warriors, of clergymen, of battlefields and victories that give honor and renown to the Scotch-Irish
name. All, however, has not been said. There is another chapter of
our history which can never be forgotten, and over it may be placed
the bold head-lines: *The Power behind the Throne, that is greater than
the Throne itself.*

What shall be said of the women of the Scotch-Irish blood? Glorious women are they. They suffered; they endured; they toiled; they
struggled; they encouraged; they prayed; they comforted. They were
wounded; they were sabered; they were murdered; they died like heroes; they were faithful to their country; they were faithful to their
sires, their husbands, and their sons. They have made Scotch-Irishmen
the best blood in the world.

In this presentation of the important and distinguished part taken
by the Scotch-Irish in bringing the struggle for American Independence to a successful issue, we would express the highest admiration for
the illustrious part borne by others in securing this common heritage.

In the first great crisis of the Revolution, when the sacred cause of
our liberties seemed to tremble in the balance, men of Scotch-Irish
blood threw themselves into the breach, and struck a blow that made
Saratoga immortal. At a later period, when the enemy had overrun the

* Headley's "Chaplains and Clergy of the Revolution," pages 230, 231.

Southland and were proudly boasting that the end was near, the brave sons of Ulster gave a lesson in the science of war at King's Mountain, at the Cowpens, and at Guilford Court-house, which taught the British Crown that not a foot of American soil had been conquered, after all the seven years' warfare. And when the "Articles of Peace" were signed, the Western boundaries of the United States were lifted from the top of the Alleghanies to the banks of the Mississippi, and because a handful of daring Scotch-Irishmen had said with their rifles: "It must be so."

And still another word must be written, which reflects imperishable honor upon the noble character of this people. In the dark days of Valley Forge, when Washington was sorely tried, and his spirit heavily burdened, when men in the Congress and in the army, who should have held up his hands, were combining to accomplish his removal, thanks to the God of the brave, no Scotch-Irishman ever laid the weight of a feather upon the troubled heart of their country's chieftain. Everywhere, in the Congress, in the army, in the gloomiest days of the Revolution, this patriotic people stood by their great commander, until he returned his commission into the hands of those who gave it, with its sacred trust gloriously accomplished. And in after days, when times of peace had come, and Virginia was prompted to give to Gen. Washington a testimonial of her appreciation of his distinguished services, he received it; but, turning to the Scotch-Irishmen of the Valley of Virginia, who had stood by him in his darkest hours, he presented the entire donation to them for their "Liberty Hall," that their sons might be educated in the principles of their noble sires.

When the great Revolution of 1776 was brought to a successful termination, and the British Government recognized the independence of the United States, the American people found themselves confronted with a profound problem full of difficulties and dangers. A better organized and more efficient government must be constructed, while the eyes of the nations are looking upon the bold venture with intense concern. The outside pressure of a common enemy being removed, the thirteen colonies felt for the first time the full meaning of their individual independence and sovereignty. The experience of a few years very clearly demonstrated that the "Articles of Confederation" were not sufficient as a bond of government between the States. The army had been disbanded, Congress was powerless to execute its regulations, and sectional jealousies were rife. It was a critical period, and strong men trembled as they looked into the future. But behind the cloud the hand of an all-wise Providence was steadily guiding the destinies of the American people.

2

On the 14th of May, 1787, a Convention of all the States was assembled at Philadelphia to construct a better and more satisfactory government, which should effectually secure to the people their rights and liberties and create a stronger bond of union. It was a sublime spectacle, the like of which had never filled any page of human history. The Convention was a body of great and disinterested men, who fully realized the difficult and responsible task before them. Mr. Curtis, in his able work on the Constitution, says: "There were men in that assembly whom for genius of statesmanship and for profound speculation in all that relates to the science of government the world has never seen overmatched." *

Washington was unanimously made the President of the Convention, a position scarcely less important than that of commander of the American armies. In accepting the position he addressed a few words to the delegates with great candor and solemnity, urging integrity in the work before them, and closed with the impressive utterance: "The event is in the hands of God." The deliberations of the Convention were continued consecutively until the 17th of September, a period of about four months, when that immortal instrument, the Constitution of the United States, was concluded, adopted, and sent to the several States for their ratification. The members were awe-struck at the result of their counsels: the Constitution was a nobler work than any one of them had believed it possible to devise.

After a century's history we see the wonderful wisdom with which they builded. Mr. Gladstone, the great English statesman, speaking of the American Constitution, says that it is "the most wonderful work ever struck off at a given time by the brain and purpose of man." Mr. Alexander Stephens, one of the profoundest writers on the American government, speaking of the framers of the Constitution, refers to them as "the ablest body of jurors, legislators, and statesmen that has ever assembled on the continent of America." The Constitution formed at this period is often spoken of as a compromise measure. This is true only in a certain sense. All were agreed that the new general government must have granted such powers as will give it efficiency and support; all else must be reserved to the States. The distribution and linking together in the best regulated form these several powers were matters of compromise. In working out this difficult problem of the constitutional government for the American people, men of Scotch-Irish blood bore a distinguished part, for they were well

* "Curtis on the Constitution," Volume I., page 387.

and ably represented in that body of intellectual giants. Alexander
Hamilton, James Wilson, and John Rutledge were of this people, and
they were three of the most conspicuous leaders in the Convention,
their extraordinary abilities all lying in different directions. After an
elaborate discussion of the principal matters which were in some way
to be embodied in the Constitution, Mr. Rutledge was appointed
chairman of a committee of five to make the first draft of this wonderful instrument.* Mr. Bancroft, speaking of this important committee,
the majority of which were of Scotch-Irish ancestry, takes occasion to
say of Mr. Rutledge: "That he was the foremost statesman of his
time south of Virginia. He was the pride of his State, and always
looked to whenever the aspect of affairs was the gravest. In the darkest hours he was intrepid, hopeful, inventive of resources, and resolute,
so that timidity and wavering disappeared before him." † Patrick Henry pronounced him the most eloquent man in the Congress of 1774.
The logical structure and frame-work of the Constitution is in a large degree the work of Mr. Rutledge, giving immortal honor to his name and
race. When shortly afterward the Constitution was before the State
Convention of Pennsylvania for adoption, Mr. Wilson, being a member of the body, made the most powerful and comprehensive analysis
of its principles and powers that has ever yet been heard.‡ It was Mr.
Hamilton's brilliant abilities that won over New York to the adoption of the Constitution. The indorsement of Rutledge carried the
matter before the Convention of South Carolina.

Mr. Madison, who took such an active part in the construction of
the Constitution, and was so closely allied with Mr. Hamilton in securing its adoption by the country, has been sometimes denominated a
Scotch-Irishman by faith. He was most thoroughly imbued with the
ideas and opinions of this people. To quote Mr. Bancroft again, he
speaks repeatedly of Mr. Madison as being a thorough disciple of Dr.
Witherspoon, of Princeton, by whom he was educated. He is an il-
lustration of the fact that the teacher sometimes re-appears with conspicuous power in his pupil. Mr. Madison is not the only student who
came away from Princeton having his whole being permeated by the
instructions received from the master spirit presiding there. The profound principles of civil and religious liberty could almost be felt in
the atmosphere of Princeton.

---

* Elliot's "Debates," pages 216, 217.
† Bancroft's "History of the United States," Volume VI., page 274.
‡ Elliot's "Debates," Volume II., pages 418–529.

In April, 1789, the government of the United States was organized, and Washington for the third time was called to take the headship of the affairs of his country; and when Chancellor Livingston administered the oath of office and cried, " Long live George Washington, President of the United States! " the earth shook with loud huzzas, and there flashed through the heavens the words of the Hebrew prophet, that " a nation shall be born at once." In that auspicious hour the principles of constitutional liberty lifted up their gorgeous structure to the gaze of an astounded world, and freedom, putting aside her battlerent garments, was peacefully wedded to the hearts of three millions of American freemen. It was a glorious day, full of thrilling interest, and radiant with anticipations for the future; and yet there lurked in many hearts a tinge of anxiety lest all might not go well as the new " Ship of State " loosed from her moorings.

But he whose hand was upon the helm chose wisely his counselors. Mr. Jefferson was chosen Secretary of State; Alexander Hamilton, Secretary of the Treasury; Henry Knox, Secretary of War; Randolph, of Virginia, Attorney-general. Rutledge, Wilson, Blair, and Iredell were appointed Associate Justices for the Supreme Court. Distinguished sons were they all of that noble race who by their courageous lives for their country and their God have made Scotland and Ireland famous forever.

On the assembling of the first Congress in April, 1789, under the new Constitution, it was found that a large number of the States had proposed a series of amendments, and the first of these was to the effect that " Congress shall make no law respecting the establishment of religion." The separation of the Church and State is universally regarded as one of the most remarkable features of the government of the United States. This great triumph in favor of religious liberty was not secured without a fierce struggle. Some maintained that the Christian religion should have the protection and support of the State. Others held to the conviction that the Protestant religion in some of its forms should be established by law. So soon as the separate colonies began organizing independent State governments it was evident that this question would have to be met. In October, 1776, the Scotch-Irish people of Virginia brought this question in a clear, distinct issue before the Legislature of Virginia in an able memorial to that body from the Presbytery of Hanover. The paper had been prepared with care, and went straight to the mark. It produced a profound impression. It was the first meeting of the Legislature as an independent State, and many foresaw that religious establishment was doomed.

In April, 1777; May, 1784; October, 1784; and August, 1785, this Presbytery of Hanover presented additional memorials of great ability on the same subject. Mr. Jefferson, in 1779, presented to the Legislature his famous bill establishing religious freedom. It was a bold enunciation of a grand principle, important to Church and State alike. In what way the author reached his wonderful conclusions he has not intimated. He had before him, however, the able memorials of the Hanover Presbytery, which discussed the whole question in the most exhaustive manner. On the 10th of January, 1786, the bill became a law, and the victory for religious freedom was won. Mr. Madison advocated the bill in a speech of great ability; and when it was passed, he said: "In Virginia was extinguished forever the ambitious hope of making laws for the human mind."

"The principle on which religious liberty was settled in Virginia prevailed at once in Maryland. In every other State oppressive statutes concerning religion fell into disuse, and were gradually repealed. This statute of Virginia, translated into French and Italian, was widely circulated through Europe." *

The demand of the first Congress for an amendment prohibiting any establishment of religion was a result brought about by the protracted and fierce struggle in the Virginia Legislature.

To the Scotch-Irish people is due the distinguished honor of ingrafting the profound principle into the government of the United States: *A free Church within a free State.* As far back as 1729 they demanded that all expressions in the Constitution of their Church referring to the exercise of powers by the civil magistrate in ecclesiastical affairs should be stricken out. And when the colonies threw off their allegiance to the British Crown, they raised the question at once that religion should not be established by the State in any form, leaving every one free to worship the divine Being in any manner or way they might choose. It was a glorious achievement, and it seems impossible to realize the magnitude of the blessings which it conveys.

In estimating the influence of the Scotch-Irish race in the formation of the government of the United States, there can be but one conclusion arrived at by a careful study of the history of that period, and that is that it was paramount to any other.

At the beginning of the American Revolution the blood of this race had a far wider distribution in this country than is generally supposed. Intermarriage gave a rapid intermingling with other classes of people;

* Bancroft's "History of the United States," Volume VI., page 158.

2*

and when events began to foreshadow the formation of a new government by the colonies, well-nigh half the population had this blood flowing through their veins. As a class, this people were very largely Presbyterians in their religious opinions; and thereby they became embodied into a compact and powerful Church organization, giving tremendous force and intensity to their influence. On the great questions of the day they were virtually an organized unit, converged into a burning focus; and it is not surprising that their influence was felt everywhere, giving form and character to public opinion on all these issues. Their ecclesiastical government extended into most if not all of the colonies; and their assemblies, coming together year by year, taught the lesson and exhibited the advantages of a strong, organized unity. Far across the waters the British Crown and Parliament saw what must be the inevitable outworking of these Presbyterian Synods. It was very manifest that this powerful ecclesiastical organization was rapidly educating the public mind to see the great benefits to be derived from a compact political body in resisting all encroachments upon their civil liberties. The Scotch-Irish people thoroughly understood the advantages of their Presbyterian system, and the disjointed elements of the revolutionary period felt and recognized its unifying power. There can be no question as to the fact that the American commonwealth is the outgrowth of that Presbyterian polity which was so thoroughly interwoven into the lives and convictions of the people who constructed it. If there was any one thing more obnoxious than another to the Stuarts and the Georges, who sat upon the British throne, it was Presbyterianism. To them it was the embodiment of all that was dangerous to the high prerogatives of kings: it was a fierce lion in the way when royal authority disregarded the rights and liberties of the people.

No people have ever enjoyed to a greater extent the blessings of constitutional liberty than have the people of this country; but it must not be forgotten that this blessed heritage cannot become a permanent possession if the principles which underlie the American Government are allowed to slip from the mind. It is still true that "eternal vigilance is the price of liberty." The success of the government of the United States has immeasurably overleaped the boundaries anticipated by those who laid its foundations with a trusting but trembling hand. The principles, which were ready for the using, came to their hands battle-scarred with the conflicts of centuries, but never yet had they been built up into a great constitutional government, guaranteeing to millions of freemen their rights and liberties under law. This grand

and immortal work was accomplished by our fathers, and blessed be their memories to the latest generation!

It is a surprising fact that no elaborate and exhaustive work has yet been written upon the American Government, although it is the great wonder of the nations. The work of Mr. Curtis, Mr. Frothingham, and Prof. Johnston, while useful and attractive, are mainly historical. The learned work of Judge Story has the nature of a legal interpretation of the Constitution as the fundamental law of the land. By far the ablest and most comprehensive treatise on the Constitution and Government of the United States is written by Mr. Calhoun. No man gave more profound thought to the principles and genius of the government of this country, and it is greatly to be regretted that he did not live to revise and prepare his work for publication himself. DeTocqueville, the eminent French statesman and political philosopher, in his "Democracy in America," has produced a very able work on American Government and institutions. He has shown a very keen and philosophic perception of the varied characteristics of the government and its workings with the people. He saw, as by intuition, the deep rootings of some of its fundamental principles, as is seen in the following utterances: "The most profound and capacious minds of Rome and Greece were never able to reach the idea, at once so general and so simple, of the common likeness of men, and of the common birthright of each to freedom." He also said: "The advent of Jesus Christ upon earth was required to teach that all the members of the human race are by nature equal and alike." *

The American Government is generally believed to be a legitimate outgrowth of the English Government in its general features, only such changes being made as were required to give it a republican form. That the Constitution and the Government of the United States owe much to "Magna Charta" and the "Bill of Rights," is certainly true; but the profound principles of this wonderful structure are much older than this. They have the strength and vigor of centuries, and find their first announcement from Mount Sinai, where the great Hebrew commonwealth was framed and given to the Hebrew people as a direct revelation from God himself. That was the only civil government which the divine Being has ever formed for the human family. He gave the Ten Commandments as a written Constitution, and gave besides a code of specific laws to govern the daily life. It was a perfect government; needed no amendments; nothing was to be repealed; noth-

---

* DeTocqueville's "Democracy in America," Volume II., page 15.

ing was to be added. The people immediately organized under it, and
all went well. The Hebrews had a population of about two millions;
the American people had about the same. The Hebrews were divided
into twelve tribes, each with a definite territory and a specific government; the Americans were divided into thirteen tribes or colonies, each
with a definite territory and a specific government. The twelve tribes
formed a federal government, known as the Hebrew commonwealth;
the thirteen colonies formed a federal government, known as the
American commonwealth. These are the only two governments in
human history which came into existence at once, and under a written
Constitution. They are the two best governments the race has ever
enjoyed. Moses was the first head of the one, Washington was the
first head of the other, and the divine Being the recognized Head and
Author of both. It would seem that there is here something more than
similarity. The principles which enter into the structure of the one
enter into the structure of the other: they are both republics.

This wonderful Hebrew commonwealth was located by the divine
Being at the confluence of three continents, and was set upon a hill to
be the light of the world for all time. The nations which came in con-
tact with the Hebrews borrowed from them in many things. Gale, in
his celebrated work, " The Court of the Gentiles," * shows conclusively
how liberally the Greeks borrowed from Moses, both as to laws and
philosophy. Solon and Plato were evidently conversant with the
writings of Moses.

The Twelve Tables of the Romans were confessedly borrowed from the
Grecian legislation, and so linked with the Mosaic laws. Both ancient
and modern writers of Roman history state that the individuals com-
missioned by the Senate and Tribune to form the Twelve Tables were
directed to examine the laws of Athens and the Grecian cities. Such
a procedure was but natural, that the written laws of older nations
should be examined in framing a new code of laws for the Roman Government. Sismondi, in his " History of the Fall of the Roman Em-
pire," † mentions the fact that " when Alfred the Great ordered a repub-
lication of the Saxon laws he had inserted several laws taken from the
Judaical ritual into the statutes." The same author states that " one
of the first acts of the clergy under Pepin and Charlemagne of France
was to introduce into the legislation of the Franks several of the
Mosaic laws found in the books of the Pentateuch." The learned

---

*Wines's " Laws of the Ancient Hebrews," pages 336, 337.
†Spring's " Obligation of the World to the Bible," pages 76, 77.

Michaelis, Professor of Law in the University of Gottinger, remarks that "a man who considers laws philosophically, who would survey them with the eye of a Montesquieu, would never overlook the laws of Moses." The able historian, Millman, in his " History of the Jews," speaking of Moses, and the wide acquaintance with his writings among other nations, affirms, that " the Hebrew law-giver has exercised a more extensive and permanent influence over the destinies of man-kind than any other individual in the annals of the world." That the succeeding ages, as well as those that were contemporaneous, were deeply indebted to Mosaic institutions, is unquestionably true. Moses himself foresaw this, and labored to impress the thought upon his countrymen as a powerful motive for the careful observance of their institutions. " Keep therefore " said he, " and do them; for this is your wisdom and your understanding in the sight of the nations, which shall hear of all these statutes, and say, Surely this great na-tion is a wise and understanding people." * The distinguished writers of every country, who have written elaborately of the fundamental laws of society, which secure individual rights and protect the personal interest of all parties, refer almost without exception to the Hebrew government and its institutions as the original source of all such laws. Beyond all question, the Hebrew commonwealth is the background, out of which has been brought the greatest and most perfect human structure the world has ever seen—*the American commonwealth.*

The American people obtained their ideas of liberty and right di-rectly from the word of God; they knew there was no mistake in the teaching, and this made them courageous and determined in the strug-gle for their liberties.

The framers of the American Government often in their writings speak of the natural right, which belongs to all men, and were possibly unconscious of the source of the great idea. Gratian, the distinguished Puritan writer, in defending natural right, said: " He termeth it that which the books of the law and the gospel do contain." The people who founded the government of the United States were thoroughly conversant with the word of God, and they thoroughly understood its infallible teachings as to the rights of men. The Bible is the original and true foundation of our American government. People in other lands have made this important discovery. Montesquieu has said: " Christianity is a stranger to despotic power." † DeTocqueville, an-

* Deuteronomy, chapter iv. 6.
† Spring's "Obligation of the World to the Bible," page 91.

other brilliant and instructive writer, says of the religion of the gospel:
" It is the companion of liberty in all its battles and all its conflicts;
the cradle of its infancy, and the divine source of its claims." *

The people of Scotch-Irish blood, who wielded such a powerful influence in the formation of the government of the United States, were
a people whose lives and being were permeated with the teachings of
the word of God. From that divine source they gathered the profound
principles of civil and religious liberty, which they were determined to
assert and maintain at any and every cost. The blessings and privi-
leges which are enjoyed under the administration of the constitutional
government of our country teach in a most conspicuous way the value
of the principles which enter into its structure. But when it is seen
that these principles of human right and liberty are grounded in the
word of God, that they are in reality a direct revelation from the divine Mind, they take on a value and measure of excellence which can
only be measured by the purposes of the great God himself.

With what watchfulness and care should the citadel of American
liberties be guarded! Here in this heaven-favored land shines the
light, the glorious light of constitutional liberty, which is to lighten
the world.

Never, never, to the latest day, can America forget the precious
blood of Ulster's sons. In the conflict for freedom they were conspicuous for unfaltering fidelity and indomitable courage. In that critical
hour, when a constitutional government was to be formed, the genius
and spirit of this wonderful people led the way; and when the amazing
structure was complete, Providence wrote the words upon the pages of
human history that Scotch-Irishmen had come to America for such a
time as this.

* Spring's " Obligation of the World to the Bible," page 91.

INVENTORS OF THE SCOTCH-IRISH RACE
OF AMERICA.

THE INVENTORS OF THE SCOTCH-IRISH RACE.

In the year 1856 a very remarkable book was published by Rev. Mr. Blakely, a Scottish clergyman, which bore the striking title: "The Theology of Inventions." He maintains, with great force, the proposition that there is a divine providence in all inventions. His argument is a strong one, characterized by much ability and research. He claims that God has bestowed all the powers possessed by the inventor; that he is the creator of the material world out of which every invention is produced, and so there must be a divine providence in all inventions, as they appear in human history.

The endowments of the human mind, as well as the nature and laws of matter, being qualities bestowed by a wise and beneficent Creator, they cannot legitimately be divorced from the designs had in view by their author.

If human life in all generations is under the guidance of divine providence, then all inventions and discoveries, which so modify and change the currents and developments of human life can no longer be considered as matters of accident, but results, which find their birth and advent at times when the greater good would accrue to humanity. He who studies carefully the problems of human history, how certain people are prepared for great eras, when wonderful achievements are gained and the interests of mankind are widened and enlarged, will be constrained to admit the statement as true that there is a Theology in Inventions.

The question may be asked, and with much significance, why were the great inventions and discoveries, which have been such a blessing to mankind, not found out until these modern days? If all inventions and discoveries have the hand of an all-wise Providence behind them, why was their advent so long delayed; and when they did come, why were they so largely developed out of a particular people, commonly known as the Anglo-Saxon race? These are questions full of interest to the thoughtful and investigating mind, and open up fields of research which have as yet been but little explored. Such problems, however, cannot be discussed on this present occasion.

It is a proverb of much broader meaning than many suppose that "necessity is the mother of invention." The demands of society, of commerce, and of civilization, have generally indicated the direction in which inventive skill should direct its energies. The greatest achievements of inventors have usually been the greatest blessings to humanity. It is preëminently true that inventors deserve well of their fellow-men. They are the great benefactors of their race. Many of them have had to struggle through great poverty, trials, and ridicule before success could be obtained. It is a sad and painful reflection upon our race that some of the greatest inventors have had their inventions filched from their hands, enriching multitudes and even nations, while they themselves have died in poverty and neglect. Suffering, penury, and martyrdom have been the only rewards for some of the most useful inventions of the world. It seems incredible that these great benefactors of the human family should have received such recompense at the hands of their fellow-men.

With these general remarks upon the subject of inventions, we invite attention to some prominent Inventors of the Scotch-Irish race. This remarkable people are not less distinguished in the art of invention than in other prominent characteristics which have marked their history.

•

ROBERT FULTON.

It will ever be a proud boast of Scotch-Irishmen that Robert Fulton was of that blood. To Mr. Fulton belongs the distinguished honor of applying the power of steam successfully to water navigation. This wonderful invention revolutionized the transportation and commerce of the world. Its beneficial effects to all nations no language could possibly estimate. It opened up the grandest era of human history, and gave such an impulse to the work of civilization as had never been known before.

Robert Fulton was born in Little Britain, Lancaster County, Pa., 1765. He was of respectable, though not wealthy family. His father and mother were of Scotch-Irish blood. Their families were supposed to be a part of the great emigration from Ireland in 1730–31. The Fulton family were probably among the early settlers of the town of Lancaster, as the father of Robert Fulton was one of the founders of the Presbyterian Church of that place. The early training of Robert Fulton was entirely in the hands of his mother, and his noble and exemplary life told how faithful she had been to her trust. The father died when his son Robert was only three years of age. The mother gave him as good an English education as her circumstances would permit, and then secured for him an apprenticeship with a prominent jeweler in Philadelphia. Here the splendid career of Fulton began. His genius for mechanics and painting was early exhibited. His hours of recreation were spent either in the mechanic's shop or in the studio with his pencil. With his first earnings he procured for his mother a comfortable home, showing the value he set upon her care and concern in his behalf. His power as an artist developed rapidly, and he was persuaded to go to London and become a pupil of Mr. West, who was then one of the most famous artists of the day, and an American. He was most favorably received by Mr. West, and so impressed was he with the promising talent of his pupil that he took him to his own home, where he enjoyed the instruction of this great master for several years.

But the drift of Mr. Fulton's genius lay in another direction. He could not be content in the artist's studio, however promising might be the result. He is soon found associated with the Duke of Bridgewater and Lord Stanhope, in making important improvements in the canal system of England. It is about this time, 1793, that Mr. Fulton first conceived the idea of propelling river boats and seagoing vessels by steam power, and in some of his manuscripts he speaks with great confidence of its practicability. The broad question of navigation and commerce in their international aspects occupied much of his thoughts, and he wrote some elaborate treatises, urging the English and French governments to give their attention to these matters as a means of developing and promoting the prosperity of this country and people. The one question which predominated in his mind all the while as he elaborated his various inventions was: Will the happiness and prosperity of the people be thereby promoted?

Before Mr. Fulton gave his entire attention to mastering the problem of steam power navigation, he applied all his energies to the production of a diving boat to destroy war vessels, after the manner of torpedoes of the present day. The invention proved quite successful, and, believing he had produced a new and important addition to naval warfare, he offered his invention to the English government. His proposition was met by a proposal, for a considerable reward, to suppress his inventions, so that neither his own country nor any other might receive the advantage. He indignantly rejected the overture, and replied with much feeling: "I will never consent to let these inventions lie dormant, should my country at any time have need for them; and were you to grant me an annuity of twenty thousand pounds a year, I would sacrifice all to the safety and independence of my country." These were noble and patriotic utterances of Mr. Fulton, and indicate the strong integrity of character which he possessed.

The career of Mr. Fulton had now reached one of its important turning points. Thoroughly discouraged at the reception which the English and French Governments had given to his inventions, he determined to return to his own country and give all his energies to the application of steam power to navigation. It was fortunate for America that adversity drove her worthy son back to her shores, as the splendid triumph of his genius was near at hand which was to reflect much glory upon himself and his country.

In the year 1806 Mr. Fulton arrived in New York, and immediately began the construction of a boat which was to test the practicability of the invention he had carefully worked out in his own mind. In less than a year, boat, engines, and machinery were all ready for the experimental trip. The boat was named "Clearmont."

after the home of Chancellor Livingston, who was associated with Mr. Fulton in this steam power experiment. In the month of August, 1807, Mr. Fulton made the public announcement that he would, on a certain afternoon, start on his new boat for Albany. At the appointed time a large multitude assembled, perfectly incredulous as to the success of the experiment. Jest and ridicule were freely expressed about "Fulton's folly." A few personal friends were invited aboard the boat to witness the trial of the new power. At the signal the vessel moved smoothly out into the midst of the river, like a thing of life, and started majestically on her trip of one hundred and fifty miles to Albany. The multitude were filled with blank amazement as the "Clearmont" disappeared from their view upon the Hudson. The crews on the sailing crafts were appalled as they saw the terrible object coming toward them belching fire and smoke; some hid themselves in the holds of the vessels, some leaped into the water and made for the shore, others fell upon the deck and implored divine protection from the approaches of the horrible monster. The people of Albany and the Legislature were filled with wonder and astonishment as the boat moved in proud majesty up to the wharf.

The following day the new vessel returned safely to New York. It was a glorious day for Mr. Fulton. His wonderful genius had triumphed over all obstacles, and the application of steam power to navigation was an established fact. It was the dawn of a new era in the prosperity of nations, and the beginning of a new period in the civilization of the world. Mr. Fulton could not be otherwise than greatly gratified at his success, but he was thinking of the welfare of his countrymen in the hour of triumph. Listen to his own noble words as he gives an account of the matter to a friend: "Having employed much time, money, and zeal in accomplishing this work, it gives me great pleasure to see it fully answer my expectations. It will give cheap and quick conveyance to the merchandise of the Mississippi, Missouri, and other great rivers, which are now laying open their treasures to the enterprise of our countrymen; and, although the prospect of personal emolument has been some inducement to me, yet I feel infinitely more pleasure in reflecting on the immense advantages that my country will derive from the invention." There is a grand nobility in these words which should touch the heart of every American citizen.

The genius and ability of Mr. Fulton entitled him to take rank among the greatest men of the world. He possessed a rare and wonderful combination of extraordinary qualities. He was one of nature's noblemen. Through his inventions he became a great benefactor to his race, reflecting honor upon his country and immortality upon himself.

His splendid career was cut short at high noon. Enthused with marvelous conceptions to reconstruct the navy of his country with the new steam power he had discovered, the energies of his delicate nature were overtaxed, and he fell a victim to disease on February 4, 1815, in his fiftieth year.

The Scotch-Irish race have great reason to be proud of the name of Robert Fulton. His wonderful genius and splendid achievements would be an honor to any people.

.

SAMUEL FINLEY BREESE MORSE

is the second distinguished inventor of the Scotch-Irish race to whom your attention is invited. Prof. Morse was born in Charleston, Mass., on April 27, 1791. He was the son of Rev. Jedediah Morse, a prominent minister of the Congregational Church of New England. His mother was Elizabeth Ann Breese, of New York City, the granddaughter of Rev. Dr. Samuel Finley, a distinguished Scotch-Irish clergyman, and an honored President of Princeton College. Prof. Morse belongs to the Scotch-Irish race through his mother, and there is no better channel through which to get the blood. By both sides of the family he had a line of ancestry remarkable for their superior intellectual endowments and culture, as well as their nobleness and integrity of character. His future life exhibited the fact that he was worthy of his noble heritage and honored sires.

The father relates the interesting incident that Rev. Dr. Witherspoon, the successor of Dr. Finley as President of Princeton College, came on a visit to him sometime after the birth of the son, and being much affected by the interview with the granddaughter of his predecessor, he took the infant son in his arms, and, looking up to God, invoked the divine benediction upon the life of the child. It was a touching scene, which the father and mother never forgot. They little dreamed, however, of the amazing blessings which were to come to the world through that life which then received the benediction of the man of God.

The early education of young Samuel Finley Morse was watched over very carefully by his father. At the age of fifteen he was fully prepared to enter the Freshman Class of Yale College in 1807, under the presidency of Dr. Timothy Dwight, who was his father's close personal friend. He was confided to Dr. Dwight's special care, and for four years he was under the molding influence of this extraordinary man. It was while at college, attending the lectures of Prof. Day on electricity, that young Morse received the seed thought which ultimately produced the great invention. In one of his morning lectures, Prof. Day gave this proposition: "If the circuit be interrupted, the fluid will become visible; and when it passes, it will leave an impression upon any intermediate body." The professor gave experiments, demonstrating the truthfulness of the proposition. This was the germ of the great invention that now daily and hourly astonishes the world, and has given a splendid immortality to the student, who, twenty-two years afterward, conceived the idea of making this experiment of practical value to mankind.

Writing in 1867 of the time when the idea of his invention first originated with him, he refers to this morning lecture at Yale College, and says: "The fact that the presence of electricity can be made visible in any desired part of the circuit was the crude seed which took root in my mind and grew up into form, and ripened into the invention of the electric telegraph."

In the summer of 1810 Mr. Samuel Finley Morse finished his collegiate course, and determined to devote himself to the art of painting, as he had already shown decided gifts in that direction. The celebrated Washington Allston had just returned from Europe in the midst of his splendid career, and young Morse was placed under his care as his pupil. In the summer of 1811 Mr. Allston returned to London, taking with him his pupil, Mr. Morse, whom he presented to Benjamin West, the great American artist, who was then President of the Royal Academy of England. Mr. West became greatly interested in Mr. Morse, and gave him the warm personal attention of a father. The young artist made rapid advancement in his profession. In less than two years he was awarded the gold medal for one of his productions, and in the presence of the royal court received the honor at the hands of the Duke of Norfolk.

After four years' absence, Mr. Morse returned to his own country, continuing his profession as an artist in different cities from 1815 to 1829. During the years 1827–28, Mr. Morse gave special attention to the study of electro-magnetism, under the inspiring lectures of Prof. Dana, of Columbia College, of New York City. His mind was still struggling with the electric force as to some method of utilizing it.

In 1829 he determined to spend some time in Italy, studying the great masters, that he might the more thoroughly perfect himself in his profession. His visit to Italy and adjacent countries, making a study of the magnificent gems of art collected in the different galleries, was a source of great pleasure and profit to him, and, richly furnished with material for future use in his profession, he determined in the fall season of 1832 to return to his own country.

Mr. Morse was now forty-two years of age. For twenty years and more he had given his entire attention to art and studies as a painter, and had attained very high distinction. But his career as an artist was now virtually at an end. His future was to be engaged in grappling with one of the grandest conceptions that ever entered the human mind.

On October 1. 1832. Mr. Morse sailed from Havre on the packet ship "Sully," for New York. There were quite a number of prominent people aboard the vessel. When fully out upon the sea, the conversation at the dinner table on a certain day turned upon electro-magnetism, and was carried on with much interest by several parties. At a particular point in the conversation Mr. Morse interposed the remark: "If the presence of electricity can be made visible in any part of the circuit, I see no reason why intelligence may not be transmitted instantaneously by electricity." Promiscuous conversation went on. But the one new idea had taken complete possession of the mind of Mr. Morse. It was as sudden and pervading as if at that moment he had received an electric shock. He withdrew from the table and went on deck. He was in midocean. His whole being was absorbed with the new conception. The purpose to transmit intelligence by electricity took possession of his mind, and to its perfection his life from that moment was devoted. The mechanism by which the result was to be reached was to be wrought out by a slow and laborious thought and experiment, but the grandeur of that result broke upon him as clearly and fully as if it had been a vision from heaven. Difficulties afterward rose in his path, which had to be surmounted or removed by toilsome and painful processes. But in that first hour of conception, when his mind was all aglow with his new discovery, he saw the end from the beginning. Of all the great inventions that has made their authors immortal, and conferred enduring benefit upon mankind, no one was so completely grasped at its inception as this. For some days and nights he had no rest or sleep, struggling with the difficult problem. His mind was all on fire. The tension of thought was very great, but he found the solution. His notebook shows that he then constructed the alphabet of dots and dashes, and the needful mechanism whereby these signs were to be made by the electric current. From this hour began a struggle which lasted twelve years, more severe, heroic, and triumphant than the annals of any other invention furnished for the warning and encouragement of genius.

As the vessel neared the wharf at New York. Capt. Pell says, Mr. Morse addressed him and said: "Well, Captain, should you hear of the telegraph one of these days as the wonder of the world, remember the discovery was made upon the good ship 'Sully.'"

Several years were spent in constructing, improving, and perfecting the mechanism of the invention. His limited supply of means became virtually exhausted. It was the old story repeated, and to be repeated, of genius struggling with poverty.

In 1838 Mr. Morse had so far perfected his invention that he proposed to make a public exhibition of the operation of telegraphic instruments at New York University, of which he was at that period a professor. On January 24, 1838, the distinguished parties invited were present, filled with astonishment at the proposition to convey intelligence through a coil of wire ten miles long. In deference to Gen. Cummings, a military officer present, the following sentence was given to Prof. Morse to transmit through the long wire in the telegraphic alphabet of dots and dashes:

"Attention, the universe:
By kingdoms, right wheel."

Letter by letter and word by word the entire sentence was written, and repeated four times over with perfect accuracy. The audience were amazed and overwhelmed. The work seemed to border on the miraculous. This is the first sentence ever transmitted through a telegraph wire of any length. The original message is still in the possession of the Cummings family. The sentence was perhaps given playfully, without the thought of any particular significance, and yet all present felt, somehow, that they stood upon the threshold of an event that would command the attention of the world, and they were not mistaken.

On February 21, 1838, Prof. Morse exhibited his telegraphic invention before the President of the United States and his cabinet and many of the members of Congress. The claims of the invention were generally regarded as utterly incredible, but when the experiment was witnessed all were compelled to admit that the telegraph had all the appearance of success.

Several years were now spent in securing grants of letters patent in foreign countries. On March 3 the Congress of the United States appropriated $30,000 to construct an experimental telegraph line from Washington to Baltimore. The speeches of ridicule made by several members of Congress on the bill making this appropriation are very amusing productions in the light of the present day. The friends of Prof. Morse had to labor assiduously to secure the passage of the bill making the appropriation. Seated in the gallery of the House of Representatives, Mr. Morse watched with intense anxiety the fate of the bill, for in its success were centered all his hopes of getting his invention before the world. Trembling with agitation, he heard the roll call. The bill had a majority of eight. He and his friends were greatly rejoiced, but the bill had yet to run the gauntlet in the Senate during the few days of Congress which yet remained. March 3 came, and Mr. Morse sat in the gallery all day long. As the senate chamber was lighted, two Senators, his personal friends, came to him with the sad intelligence that there was no hope of getting the bill passed, as only a few hours remained and a large number of bills were before it on the calendar. His hopes were crushed. He went to his hotel, fell upon his knees at his bedside, and poured out his troubled heart to God, as he had ever done in the dark days when thick shadows fell upon him. He soon realized that "the Lord giveth his beloved sleep." Mr. Ellsworth, the Commissioner of Patents, and his friends in the Senate watched the bill continuously, and at the last moment secured its passage and signature by the President. Early next morning the little daughter of Mr. Ellsworth came to the hotel as Prof. Morse came down to breakfast. The young girl quickly said: "I came so early to be the first to congratulate you. Mr. Morse." "And for what reason, my child?" said he. "Why, upon the passage of the bill by the Senate." The professor assured her that it was not possible, as he left the capitol only a few hours before adjournment. She then informed him that her father was present at the close, and saw the billed passed and signed. He sank down in his chair overwhelmed at the good news. Recovering himself, he promised Miss Annie Ellsworth that she should send the first message over the first line of telegraph that was opened.

With this appropriation by Congress, Prof. Morse proceeded with energy and delight to construct a telegraph line from Washington to Baltimore. By May 24, 1844, he had his line constructed between the two cities. There was much excitement in both cities as to the success of the new and wonderful invention. That intelligent messages could be sent over this wire of forty miles' length in an instant staggered the faith of every one.

When everything was ready, he informed Miss Ellsworth he was prepared to redeem his pledge that she should indite the first message for the telegraph line. Her good mother had suggested the striking words of Scripture:

"What hath God wrought!" (Num. xxiii. 23)

and the daughter handed them to Prof. Morse. He took his seat by the instrument and spelled the words of the message in the dot and dash of the telegraph alphabet. In a moment Mr. Vail, who was at the instrument in Baltimore, returned the words to Washington, thus passing over a circuit of eighty miles.

The parties present were filled with amazement; they saw beyond controversy the success of the invention. Prof. Morse did not exhibit the surprise of his enthusiastic friends, for he knew perfectly what his instrument would do, and the fact accomplished was but the confirmation to others of what to him was a certainty on the packet ship "Sully " in 1832.

He received, with the modesty in keeping with the simplicity of his character, the strong congratulations of his friends. Neither then nor at any subsequent period of his life did his language or manner indicate any exultation in his wonderful triumph. He believed himself an instrument employed by heaven to achieve a great result, and having accomplished it, he claimed simply to be the original and only instrument by which that result had been reached.

Prof. Morse said of the first message that was sent—"What hath God wrought!"—that it baptized the American telegraph with the name of its author, who, he believed, was God.

The original slip of paper on which his first dispatch was written by the telegraph instrument is now in the possession of Gov. Seymore, of Hartford, Conn.

It was two days after the sending of this dispatch that the famous Democratic Convention of 1844 met in Baltimore. The nomination of James K. Polk for President, who was a distinguished Scotch-Irishman, was first flashed over the wires, but it seemed impossible to believe it until the train from Baltimore verified it. In the struggle over the nomination for Vice President, parties in Washington and Baltimore kept up a continual conference for hours. As these various dispatches were read every few minutes for hours before the Convention, all doubts as to the success of the electric telegraph was effectually dissipated.

The telegraph was now a reality. Its completion was hailed with universal enthusiasm. The press of the country announced the annihilation of time and space in intercourse among men. The praises of the inventor were proclaimed by every one. The wonder and joy of the people were beyond expression.

It was not long until telegraph lines were established to all the leading cities of the country. In was only a question of a short time untill all the governments of Europe adopted the Morse telegraph. Nation after nation conferred upon him their highest honors and badges of distinction. The electric telegraph was at once recognized as the most wonderful invention of human history.

The wearisome days of poverty and need were now ended; possessed with a liberal revenue from his invention, he purchased a beautiful home on the east bank of the Hudson, near Poughkeepsie. Here in comfort and ease, overwhelmed with the honors of the world, he rested from his labors. The grand triumph of his life had been achieved. Here in his beautiful home he often talked pleasantly of the dark days through which he had passed before his invention could be brought to perfection, and its merit recognized by the public. Seated in his richly furnished study, he had telegraphic communication with his friends in every part of the world.

The character of Prof. Morse was of a high order in every respect. His strong religious life exhibited itself throughout his whole career from youth to old age. When his invention brought him ample means, he made liberal benefactions to the various causes in which he felt interested.

In the summer of 1871 a statue was erected to his memory in Central Park, New York, by the Telegraphic Brotherhood of the world. At a public reception given at the Academy of Music on the occasion, when the venerable old man came upon the platform, the immense audience arose and cheered with unbounded enthusiasm. He was led to a seat beside a small table, on which was the first instrument ever used, which was connected by wire with the telegraphic system of the world. He laid his finger upon the key. There was a moment's impressive silence; then the clicking of the telegraph instrument was heard as the "Father of the Electric Telegraph" gave his farewell message:

Greeting and thanks to the telegraph fraternity throughout the world. Glory to God in the highest. On earth peace and good will to men.
S. F. B. MORSE.

From all parts of the globe came back the answers with benedictions for him who had made the people of all nations to be as one.

The career of this wonderful man now closes. On April 4, 1872, in his eighty-fourth year, the message came calling him to the precious rewards of his Christian faith.

CYRUS HALL McCORMICK.

ATTENTION is now directed to another distinguished Scotch-Irish-man, to whose genius and tenacity of purpose we are indebted for another most important invention; one which has wrought a profound revolution in the agricultural world. We refer to the wonderful and famous "McCormick Reaper," the invention of Cyrus Hall McCormick, of Chicago. This invention soon exhibited far-reaching results, affecting the agricultural interests in every land. By its use the commerce of the world, in all kinds of grain products, has been expanded to amazing proportions, and it may be safely as-serted that no single invention has ever become such a powerful factor in increasing the commerce of all nations.

The family of Cyrus Hall McCormick for two generations were settlers in the famous valley of Virginia, so fruitful of great and good men, and originally came to this country from the North of Ireland in 1758.

The homestead of Robert McCormick, the father of Cyrus Hall McCormick, was Walnut Grove, Rockbridge County, Va. Here his son was born February 15, 1809. The father had a very decided genius for invention in the line of mechanics. He was the inventor of several important machines, which in that early day were of much value to agriculture in various ways. In 1816 he conceived the idea of constructing a reaping machine. When he had built his machine and put it to the test, it failed to do satisfactory work.

Cyrus H. McCormick, the son, was now about twenty-two years of age, and he had already invented several important agricultural implements, showing that the inventive genius of the father was inherited by the son.

In the summer of 1831 he made a careful study of the problem of the reaper which had baffled the skill of his father. While stand-ing in a field of ripening and tangled grain, the solution of the diffi-cult problem seems to have flashed upon his mind at once. In a few short months he had so far constructed his machine as to sub-ject it to a critical experiment, which was done at the old homestead at Walnut Grove. The trial was a complete success, and from that day the reaper was an accomplished fact.

Mr. McCormick did not allow himself to be carried away by the

enthusiasm of his wonderful success. His critical and inventive mind soon saw where improvements could be made, rendering the machine less complicated and more efficient in its work.

For several years his father and two brothers were associated with him in the manufacture of the reaper at Walnut Grove, and year by year the success and capability of the machine was assured beyond all controversy. The want of facilities for the manufacture of the varied parts of the reaper rendered it impossible to put it upon the market with a rapidity even approximating the demand. The vast prairies of the West were rapidly becoming the great grain-producing part of the country, and Mr. McCormick, in his uncommon good judgment and foresight, saw that these broad prairies must be the field where his wonderful reaper was to have its grandest success. Accordingly in 1845 he began making his reapers in Cincinnati, but in 1847 he located permanently in Chicago, and established a large manufactory with the most improved machinery for producing his reaper with rapidity and perfection. His two brothers from Virginia joined him there, and the firm became a potent factor in building up the great Northwest.

Thousands of reapers were now manufactured and distributed over the grain-producing parts of the country. The whole land was soon filled with amazement at the tremendous commercial significance of the new invention. Reaping the harvest by machinery increased immensely the grain products of the country, and the volume of commerce was augmented year by year to a surprising degree.

Mr. McCormick now turned his attention to the introduction of his reaper into the different countries of Europe, and his efforts in this direction were crowned with abundant success. From 1851 to 1883, a period of more than thirty years, the "McCormick Reaper" took the gold medals and highest prizes of the several international expositions that were held. In 1867 Napoleon III. was present to witness a test of the merit of the reaper invention in the rich harvest fields of Chalon, and so pleased was the emperor at the wonderful success of the reaper that he conferred the Decoration of the Legion of Honor upon Mr. McCormick on the field. The Emperor of Austria conferred a like honor at the exposition of Vienna in 1873, and, indeed, from every part of the world public recognition in the form of honors and awards came to the distinguished inventor. He was permitted to see the merit of his wonderful invention recognized in all lands, and also to see its amazing influence in expanding and enlarging the commerce of the world. No one rejoiced more than he in the great advantages and blessings which his invention gave to the agricultural interests of the country. Reaping by machinery was a revolution to the grain production of the world.

The success which a kind Providence was pleased to bestow upon Mr. McCormick seemed never to fill him with exultation, but only served to bring out the remarkable excellencies of his character. In 1858 he was married to Miss Nettie Fowler, a lady distinguished for her intelligence and mental endowments. To them were born two daughters and three sons.

The religious life of Mr. McCormick was strong and of a pronounced type. He held, with vigorous tenacity, to the religious faith of his fathers. He loved his Church and all her interests, and when his inventions brought him ample fortune, he began to bestow large and liberal benefactions upon such religious institutions as commended themselves to his favorable consideration. In 1859 he endowed the Presbyterian Theological Seminary, of Chicago, and afterward large and liberal gifts were made, both by himself and his family, amounting in all to over a million dollars. After Mr. McCormick's death the Trustees of the seminary very properly changed the corporate title of the institution to that of "The McCormick Theological Seminary of Chicago." Through this liberally endowed school of the prophets this noble man has already exerted, and will continue to exert, a most favorable religious influence upon the great Northwest section of our country. Mr. McCormick died in the year 1884, having passed his seventy-fifth birthday. His end was peace.

In the person of his son, Cyrus Hall McCormick, Jr., the father has left behind him a good representative. Succeeding to his father's invention with all its emoluments, he has expanded the principles of the invention in various directions, largely increasing its influence and revenues. Just where the father laid down his life, both secular and religious, the son has taken it up, and is pressing forward with great activity and success. He is a worthy son of a noble sire.

There is a striking resemblance in the career of Mr. McCormick and that of Prof. Morse. Mr. McCormick reached the full conception of his invention after a short but close study in the summer of 1831. Prof. Morse reached the full conception of his invention after a few days of intense study on the packet ship "Sully" in October, 1832. Both inventions were a success in the first trial, and both were about twelve years in commanding public attention. Both men about the same time had their inventions recognized by the various nationalities of Europe and of the world, and almost simultaneously they received the highest honors from every civilized government. While engaged in developing their respective inventions, they formed an acquaintance which was mutually pleasant and agreeable. They both lived to enjoy the fruits of their labors, and passed away at a ripe old age, leaving behind them the blessed example of Godly Christian lives.

In preparing this address on the inventors of the Scotch-Irish people of America, we have deemed it advisable to restrict ourselves to the three great Inventors (Mr. Fulton, Mr. Morse, and Mr. McCormick), whose life work has been closed by death. The inventive genius of these three men lay in entirely different directions, and yet their inventions have effected most powerfully the interests of mankind, and proved an inestimable blessing to the whole world.

If time would permit, we could speak of other Scotch-Irish inventors whose productions have commanded universal attention and admiration. The mother of Thomas A. Edison, who was Miss Elliott, is of this blood; a woman of rare endowments and intellectual culture, who profoundly impressed herself upon the young life of her son.

But we must rest our cause with the three master Inventors we have mentioned. Their Inventions, their lives, and their characters reflect immortal honor upon the Scotch-Irish race.